The Huffin Puff Express

Express

by David L. Harrison
pictures by Art Seiden

A Golden Book · New York
Western Publishing Company, Inc.
Racine, Wisconsin 53404

H I J

The Huffin Puff Express is rolling,
Clickety, clickety-clack.
Its wheels are turning round and round,
Rumbling along the track.

Pillow clouds of fleecy steam
Are puffing from its stack . . .
Rumble, rumble,
Puff, puff,
Clickety, clickety-clack.

Seven cars of frozen food,
Twenty cars of grain,

Another twenty cars of coal,
A flatcar with a crane—

Fourteen tanker cars of oil,
A car of sugarcane,

And nineteen cars of pigs and cows
Are rolling in this train.

Steaming through the countryside,
Whistling at the sun,
Rumbling through the villages
On its daily run . . .
Three hundred fifty miles to go
Before the day is done!

Across a bridge,
Across a prairie,
Clickety, clickety-clack—

Around a bend,
Around a lake,
And past a miner's shack . . .

Through a canyon,
Through a town,
It's rumbling down the track.

Past ponies in their barnyards,
Past roosters, chicks, and hens . . .

Past cattle grazing in their pastures,
Pigs asleep in pens—

Past rabbits hopping through the clover,
Deer in shady glens.

Puffing up a mountainside,
Through fields of ice and snow . . .
Chug . . chug . . . chug . . . . chug,
Going . . . . . so . . . . . . slow—

When we finally reach the top,
Hear the whistle blow.
Puff, puff,
Toooo, toooo . . .
One hundred miles to go!

Down, down the other side,
Puffing fleecy steam . . .
Past a forest,
Past a meadow,
Past a bubbling stream—

Past a farmer in his field,
Plowing with his team . . .
Ch-ch, ch-ch,
Ch-ch, ch-ch,
Pillow clouds of steam.

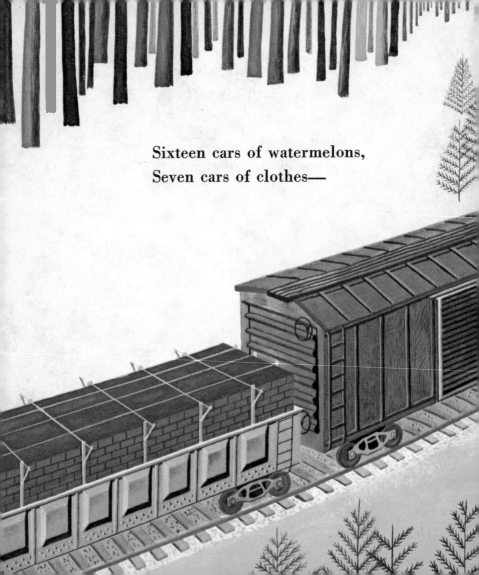

Sixteen cars of watermelons,
Seven cars of clothes—

A mail car filled with letters,
And a car of garden hose . . .

A car with seven thousand bricks
Stacked in even rows.

The Huffin Puff Express is rolling,
Rolling down the line.
The moon will soon be coming up;
It's nearly half-past nine.
The engineer is happy,
And the crew is feeling fine,
Clickety-clackety, clickety,
Clickety-clacking down the line.

Standing at the station house,
People watch and wait,
Hoping that the Huffin Puff
Doesn't come in late—
Counting on the engineer
To get there with the freight.

Where's the Huffin Puff Express?
The Huffin Puff is due.
Where's that Huffin Puff Express?
It should be coming through.

I hear the Huffin Puff Express!
Right on schedule, too . . .
Puff, puff,
Chug, chug,
Toooo, toooo, toooo!

Feel the tracks begin to tremble!
Hear the wheels ring!
Smell the pillow clouds of steam!
See the lantern swing!
The Huffin Puff Express is in!
Ding! Ding! Ding!

The engineer is climbing off.
The crew is homeward bound.

One by one, the people leave. . . .
There's not a soul around.

The Huffin Puff Express is resting.
Shhh, don't make a sound.
Shhh, shhh
  shhh
    shhh
      shhhhh. . . .
Don't make a sound.